Snow in the City

Snow in the City

A winter's tale

by Berta and Elmer Hader

The Macmillan Company, New York
Collier-Macmillan Limited, London
1963

Library of Congress catalog card number: 63-18461

FIRST PRINTING

The Macmillan Company, New York
Collier-Macmillan Canada, Ltd., Toronto, Ontario

PRINTED IN THE UNITED STATES OF AMERICA

For
Mabel C. Lucas
and her Third Grade pupils,
with appreciation of
their enthusiasm for books

This is Paul and his sister, Pamela, with their dog, Peter the Poodle. They live in the city with their mother and father. Paul's father looks like Paul. This pleases him. Paul's mother looks like Pamela. This pleases her.

This is their house in the city. Many people in the city live in apartment houses with a man to open the door and a janitor to keep everything clean. Paul's father and mother like to live in a house. So do Paul and Pamela and Peter the Poodle.

2

On Thanksgiving Day, Uncle Fred came to take Pamela and Paul to see the BIG TOY PARADE. When they left home the sky was gray and there was snow in the air. Downtown they found crowds of people waiting for the Parade.

"Here they come, Pamela," shouted Paul, as the music of the marching bands was heard in the distance. This was the big parade on Thanksgiving Day. Children and grown-ups, too, lined the sidewalks of the wide, empty street which would soon be filled with gay floats of Toyland, clowns and acrobats, marching bands, and drill teams. Paul and Pamela stared wide-eyed at the enormous balloons—a giant turkey, Santa Claus, and a great, green dragon—floating high above the heads of the paraders. Then the first snow began to fall.

4

After the Thanksgiving holiday Paul and Pamela spent busy days in the neighborhood school. The winds from the north grew colder as the Christmas season drew near. All the children hoped for a white Christmas.

Two days before Christmas, when Pamela and Paul were walking Peter the Poodle in the park, a snowflake tumbled out of the dark sky. Soon the air was filled with dancing, swirling snowflakes. The children hurried home to tell their mother the good news.

The snow fell all that night and covered the sidewalks, the
streets, and the rooftops of the sleeping city. The snow was
still falling when Pamela and Paul wakened in the morning.
This was the day before Christmas. The children shouted
with joy. It would be a white Christmas!

Pamela and Paul put on their
warm coats and snow boots. They
were going with Uncle Fred to
see the Christmas shop windows
on the Avenue. The streets were
crowded with cars and buses.

People hurried in and out of

subways. People got on and off
buses. Workers made their way to
office buildings or stores. Shoppers
crowded the sidewalks. It was fun
walking with Uncle Fred and all
the other people through the falling snow.

The windows of the stores held presents for everyone:
everything from candy, toys, clocks, and clothing to cars,

furs, and diamonds. Uncle Fred bought Pamela a walking
toy Santa Claus from a sidewalk vendor.

Pamela thought the windows showing dolls and fairy-tale puppets were the prettiest on the Avenue. Paul liked the window full of toy rockets and spaceships. Uncle Fred looked longest at the windows of the bookstores. All were gay with tinsel and holly. Many children stopped to talk to the jolly Santa Claus standing near the curb. They left Peter the Poodle at the pet shop while they had sandwiches and milk at the lunch counter. Then Uncle Fred bought tickets for the Christmas show at the Music Hall.

Paul and Pamela had a good time at the Music Hall and Uncle Fred was glad to rest after their walk. They collected Peter the Poodle. Then Paul and Pamela stopped to look at the kittens and puppies in the window of the pet shop.

Uncle Fred bought roasted chestnuts from the chestnut vendor. Hot chestnuts were just the thing for a cold day.

Snow covered window ledges, clung to church steeples, and coated the branches of trees in the streets. Paul and Pamela stopped to see the city's largest Christmas tree. A few skaters were on the Plaza rink below. The sound of Christmas carols reminded Uncle Fred that this was Christmas Eve and he had promised to bring Paul and Pamela home early.

18

The streets leading out of the city were crowded with cars full of people on their way to spend the holiday with friends in the country. Hundreds of cars brought merrymakers into the city to join gay parties in theaters, restaurants, and hotels. Pamela, Paul, and Uncle Fred rode home in a taxi through the Park.

The bare branches of the trees, already heavy with snow, sparkled under the bright lights in the Park. Pamela and Paul saw many pretty Christmas trees and windows and doorways trimmed with twinkling, colored lights. The city streets were full of song and good cheer. They stopped to listen to children singing carols near their house, while Uncle Fred paid the taxi driver and wished him a Merry Christmas.

Christmas morning Paul and Pamela found skates and mittens and a pair of skis for each of them, and other gifts, too, under their Christmas tree. They looked out the windows. Snow covered the streets and all the rooftops.

The wind blew the snow into high drifts that blocked
highways, streets, and railroad tracks leading into the city.

Trains moved slowly and were many hours late. Buses and trucks were stalled on the highways. Airplanes were grounded.

Snow is beautiful to look at and gives pleasure to many young people, but snow in the city means work, much work. The main streets must be cleared of snow so trucks loaded with fresh food and supplies for the people can reach the markets. The streets have to be cleared, too, for the city fire trucks, ambulances, garbage trucks, and buses. All the city snowplows and snow-removal trucks work day and night. Hundreds of men are hired by the city to help clear the snow away.

The day after Christmas many city workers who lived far uptown shoveled paths through the deep snow to the bus stop. But no buses were running. The snow had blown into deep drifts and blocked the streets. Until the city plows cleared their streets they were snowbound.

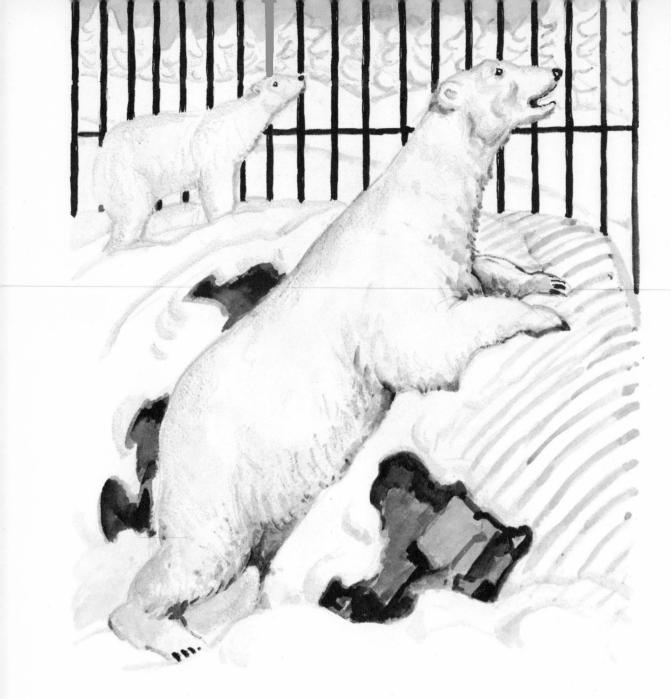

The first Saturday after Christmas all the streets were
cleared of snow, so Uncle Fred took Pamela and Paul to the
park zoo. Most of the animals preferred to be indoors on such
a cold day, but the snow on the ground brought happy mem-
ories to the polar bears and the penguins. They enjoyed the
snow and cold.

Wherever they walked, Pamela and Paul saw children tumbling in the snowdrifts in the streets and parks. School would soon begin again and they were enjoying the holiday.

They got out their sleds and their skis to use on the slopes in the park, or on side streets, before the snowplows and trucks carted all the snow away. They made snowballs and snowmen and everyone had fun in the snow.

Every Saturday, after Paul and Pamela had finished their schoolwork, they put on their snowsuits and Uncle Fred took them to the ski run in the big park far uptown. Uncle Fred was a good teacher and Paul and Pamela had fun skiing on the lower slopes.

All winter the snow lay heavy on trees, bushes, and grass in the city parks. The pigeons, other birds, and squirrels might have starved, but they had many friends in the city.

Men shoveled paths and cleared ground to feed the birds and squirrels. Paul and Pamela made many trips to the park to help feed the hungry ones.

The flocks of city pigeons, starlings, and sparrows that made their homes under the eaves and on the ledges of large buildings were hungry, too. Boys and girls and many grown-up friends scattered seeds and bread crumbs on the sidewalks near the birds' nesting places.

There was snow on the ground most of that winter. But with the coming of the warm spring sun the snow melted, and soon the trees along the streets and in the parks put out green leaves again. Winter with all the snow was gone, but Paul and Pamela knew it would come again and again to clothe the city in magic beauty, and to give joy to boys and girls.

HADER BOOKS

Big City
The Big Snow
Cock-a-Doodle-Doo
The Farmer in the Dell
The Friendly Phoebe
Home on the Range
Little Antelope
Little Appaloosa
Little Chip
The Little Stone House
The Little Town
Little Whitefoot
Lost in the Zoo
The Mighty Hunter
Mister Billy's Gun
Pancho
Quack-Quack
Rainbow's End
Reindeer Trail
The Runaways
Snow in the City
Spunky
Wish on the Moon